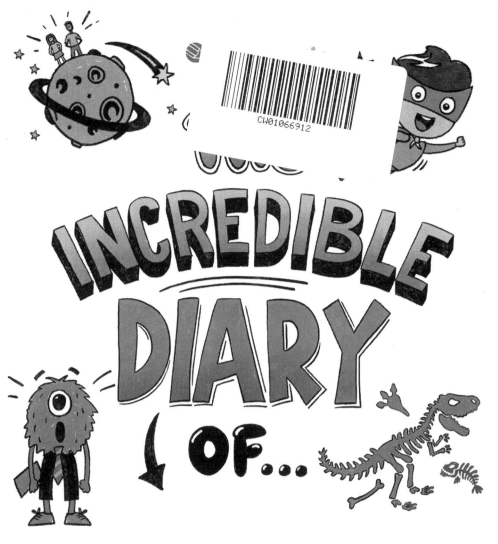

INCREDIBLE DIARY OF...

Enchanted Tales

Edited By Andy Porter

First published in Great Britain in 2023 by:

Young Writers
Remus House
Coltsfoot Drive
Peterborough
PE2 9BF
Telephone: 01733 890066
Website: www.youngwriters.co.uk

Printed and bound in the UK by BookPrintingUK
Website: www.bookprintinguk.com
YB0MA0030A

FOREWORD

Dear Diary,

You will never guess what I did today! Shall I tell you? Some primary school pupils wrote some diary entries and I got to read them, and they were EXCELLENT!

Here at Young Writers we created some bright and funky worksheets along with fun and fabulous (and free) resources to help spark ideas and get inspiration flowing. And it clearly worked because WOW!! I can't believe the adventures I've been reading about. Real people, make believe people, dogs and unicorns, even objects like pencils all feature and these diaries all have one thing in common – they are JAM-PACKED with imagination, all squeezed into 100 words!

Here at Young Writers we want to pass our love of the written word onto the next generation and what better way to do that than to celebrate their writing by publishing it in a book! It sets their work free from homework books and notepads and puts it where it deserves to be – **OUT IN THE WORLD!**

Each awesome author in this book should be super proud of themselves, and now they've got proof of their imagination, their ideas and their creativity in black and white, to look back on in years to come!

CONTENTS

Brockholes Wood ASC, Preston

Ava Evans (11)	45
Ruqaya Al-Saati (10)	46
Karrar Al-Saati (8)	47
Jake Evans (9)	48

Buxlow Preparatory School, Wembley

Megu Mizuno (11)	49

Chorlton Park Primary School, Chorlton

Dillon Bradbury (10)	50
Zayan Chowdhury (10)	51
William Harvest (10)	52

Christ Church Academy, Stone

Elodie Milward (11)	53
Alyssa-May Crowther (11)	54
Harry Norwood (10)	55
Lilly-May Dee (10)	56
Charlie Woodall (11)	57
Oliver Humphries (10)	58
Connor O'leary (11)	59
Holly McPherson (11)	60
Harry Pearsall (11)	61
Harvey Rowson (10)	62
Jessica Allinson (9)	63

Cranbrook Primary School, Ilford

Ayyub Ansari (8)	64
Inaya Haque (9)	65
Yusuf Shaikh (8)	66
Ismaeel Choudhry (9)	67
Amelia Ahmed (9)	68
Haoyu Yang (9)	69

Dothill Primary School, Wellington

Simona Yordanova (11)	70

Drummore Primary School, Stranraer

Kaylyn Marshall (11)	71

Gardners Lane Primary School, Cheltenham

Tymon (8)	72
Nurgul Aslan (9)	73
Tommy Baron (8)	74
Garvit Nagpal (8)	75
Maame Boateng-Bandoh (9)	76
Sophia White (9)	77
Adeife Aribisala (8)	78
Kochyar Garib (9)	79
Jaydon Finn (8)	80
Tyler O'Neill (9)	81
Holly Borley (8)	82
David Velescu (8)	83

Gayton CE Primary School, Gayton

Louie Garner (8)	84
Chloe To (7)	85

Greatstone Primary School, Greatstone

Darcy Taylor (7)	86
Henry-Joe Nightingale (6)	87

Greenhill Primary School, Bury

Hashim Zeeshan Zulfeqar (9)	88
Khadijah Hussain (9)	89
Elfi Jones (8)	90

Halfway Primary School, Llanelli

Jessica Wilson (9)	91
Aathana Sanjeevan (9)	92

Hatchell Wood Primary Academy, Bessacarr

Evelyn Burton (10)	93

Highfields Primary Academy, Highfields

Leo Baxter (11)	94
Leo Hollinshead (11)	95

Holy Cross Catholic Primary School, Leicester

Nancy Pious (11)	96
Jessika Rathinam (11)	97
Shylah Mordarska (10)	98
Kaleb Melia (11)	99

Ladyloan Primary School, Arbroath

Lennon Watton (7)	100

Morley Victoria Primary School, Morley

Saira Hussein-Utley (9)	101
Olivia Loney (9)	102

Mossford Green Primary School, Barkingside

Mishal Aamir (8)	103
Habiba Naeem (8)	104
Hasan Gunes (8)	105

Northcote Primary School, Liverpool

Mason Cunningham (8)	106

Iylah-May Cameron (9)	107
Mason Stanton (8)	108
Kacy McHugh (9)	109
Dennis Campbell (8)	110
Heidi Livesy (9)	111

Our Lady's RC Primary School, Perth

Lexi Cummings (10)	112

Parkfield Primary School, Hendon

Wajeeh Ather (10)	113
Darius Creivean (11)	114
Elias Vargas (10)	115
Nacer Agouni Tabac (10)	116

Pound Hill Junior School, Pound Hill

Tesh Davies (9)	117
Eesa Khan (9)	118
Angelina Wong (10)	119

Prendergast Ladywell School, Lewisham

Olive Massa (6)	120
Mimi Copeland (6)	121
Anika Paquete (11)	122

Riddlesden St Mary's CE Primary School And Nursery, Riddlesden

Maymunah Basharat (9)	123

Springfield Primary Academy, Scartho

Olivia Soulsby (9)	124
Harry Cook (9)	125

THE STORIES

The Humans Who Went To Saturn

Dear Diary,

I was one of four humans who went to Saturn. We saw four big sloppy aliens. "OMG!" I said.

"No need to get scared," said Jake.

"Yes," said Emma, "Jake is right."

"Well, I am still scared. What if they creep up on us?"

"They won't."

"Argh! They're going to gobble us up. Argh! I'm scared," I said. "I bet they are going to kill us now. Wait a second, are they just trying to say hello? They might just want to be our friends."

I put on my headphones and was able to understand him.

Alexis Grace Kinch (8)

Aberdare Town Church Primary School, Aberdare

The Planet Adventure

Once when I was walking to the shop and saw a ginormous spaceship but then the grey door opened and there was a slimy alien. I ran as fast as I could but he said, "I am not going to hurt you. I am a nice alien." He then said, "Do you want to go on a space adventure?"

"Yes please."

We then took off. He said, "What planet do you want to go to?"

"Saturn. What are those big circles around it?"

"Those are its rings."

"What planet is that?"

"It's Uranus."

"That was cool." Then I went home.

Harper Cable (8)

Aberdare Town Church Primary School, Aberdare

The Uranus Disaster

Dear Diary,

I woke up and it was 9999, 31st December 23:40. I was shocked because I was on Uranus. It was so cold and there was so much ice. I found a spaceship. I got in and saw food, a bed and water. I went to the front of the spaceship and I went back to Earth. I landed on Earth and walked back home. I knocked on the door and my mum opened it and she screamed in excitement. I felt elated.

Lylah O'Sullivan (9)

Aberdare Town Church Primary School, Aberdare

My Arsenal Trip

Dear Diary,

One day I went to the Arsenal stadium where Arsenal were playing Fulham. When the game started, I was very nervous that top-of-the-league Arsenal were playing sixth-place Fulham The game started and Fulham weren't messing about. They scored just before half-time. I was devastated that we slipped.

The second half started. Then, with thirty minutes left, Arsenal scored. I was so happy and scared because we had to win. The clock was ticking. Everyone was sweating. It was our last chance. Two minutes to go and Arsenal scored. I was so happy.

Shray Parmar (9)

Ashfield Junior School, Bushey

The New Beginning

Dear Diary,

19th of August in 1800. I was fifteen months old. A significant event occurred in my life. I was being cared for by three women while watching a horse show. A storm erupted and the three women died instantly. The woman who was holding me got struck by lightning. People that were watching rushed to help. They rushed me to my parents and put me in hot water. After the lightning, I was thought to be a sickly, quiet child but the lightning gave me a new beginning. It was amazing that I survived the terrible lightning strike.

Maya Mehta (9)

Ashfield Junior School, Bushey

The Ichthyosaurus

Dear Diary,
I found an amazing ichthyosaur skull which was one of my first big finds. I found the ichthyosaur in Lyme Regis where the Jurassic Coast is. The ichthyosaur, when found, came with just the skull. I saw something I'd never seen in my life. I saw a large rock that was actually a fossil. It was so big. I was super excited about my experience. I got famous. I loved this experience even though I didn't get much credit. This was something I never thought I would find, even with anyone's help. I am very proud.

Georgie Kirby (10)
Ashfield Junior School, Bushey

The Famous Tiger

Dear Diary,

Last year I went on a safari trip. I could not wait to see the famous tiger. Everyone seemed to be excited about it.

The deeper I went into the safari the more curious I became. The moonlight was shining brightly on my shoulders when I reached the cave of the tiger. While quietly approaching the entrance my heart was beating as fast as a racing car. My palms were sweaty.

There he was, the famous tiger, standing proud in front of my eyes. I was stunned by its beauty. Its image is still alive in my heart.

Lana Greyling (8)

Ashfield Junior School, Bushey

My Astonishing, Stupendous Finds

Dear Diary,
I found the colossal ichthyosaurus today. The immense ichthyosaur was a temnodontosaurus and a holotype. I sold the ichthyosaurs for £45 5s and it saved my family financially. In 1823, when I was 14 years old, I found the plesiosaur. The giant plesiosaur was a dolichodeirus but not a holotype. I sold the plesiosaur for exactly £200. I was given absolutely no credit for any of my amazing, fascinating finds. It was all given to the sluggish buyers who did none of the work at all. I was so devastated.

Rian Gurney (10)
Ashfield Junior School, Bushey

My Amazing Discoveries

Dear Diary,

I was so thrilled when I found an ichthyosaur skull. Even though I didn't get any credit for my finds I still enjoyed finding them. The men that bought the skull from me got all the credit. I sold it for £45 5s to a rich scientist. Having decided to sell the ichthyosaur skull I have made enough money to survive and have food and drink. It happened on the beach at Lyme Regis and it was hidden in a cliff. When I first saw it I was amazed by its monstrous size. I couldn't be more thrilled.

Ethan Barker (10)

Ashfield Junior School, Bushey

A Diary Account Of The Life Of Mary Anning

Dear Diary,
Today I began to remember when me and my brother found an ichthyosaur skull. I had woken up to go to the cliffs with my brother, Joseph like I normally would. It was while searching we found it. I felt extremely proud but slightly upset because my father wasn't there to celebrate the discovery. When I really miss him I think about how proud he would be. Although he isn't here, I know he would be proud of us now. When I fossil hunt I think about the special times we had.
Mary Anning.

Niamh Browne (10)
Ashfield Junior School, Bushey

Travelling In Time

Dear Diary

Me and my best friend, Rowan, always get detention but we had a big adventure on Friday. We escaped school and had lots of fun, drank Pepsi and ate Walkers. We walked along and saw a factory. We were fascinated. It was all rusty and dirty. When we went in we both felt that it was treacherous. All of a sudden, we were in the Stone Age. We saw really weird stuff and people. Then suddenly, we were straight back at the factory. We ran back to school. We told our friend about our curious adventure.

Phillip Matvejev (9)

Ashfield Junior School, Bushey

Bushi

Dear Diary,
It's another day in the mystery kingdom and I had to do some plumbing for a yellow toad. After that, I had to see the princess but when I got to the castle, she wasn't there. All that was left was a single toad. I had to save the princess. I saw my brother, Luigi. He felt brave. We got into our plumbing truck and drove off. We had lots of fun listening to the radio. We arrived at Bowser's castle and we saved the princess. We got a star and that was a happy ending.

Mason Sharkey (9)
Ashfield Junior School, Bushey

A Diary Account Of The Life Of Mary Anning

Dear Diary,

I think I might not have to live on the streets after all! Goodbye poor world, hello rich world! I felt excited and curious. When I went to the beach this morning I was looking at fossils. I saw an unusually big ammonite. I went over to the slab and started chipping away at it. As I was, the fossil was gradually getting bigger and bigger. I asked my father's old friends to carry it to my house. When I got it home, everything changed. An undiscovered species I had found...

Emily Kaye (10)
Ashfield Junior School, Bushey

Dear Diary

Dear Diary,

Some time ago I met an alien. His name was Boby. We met a long time ago. Ever since I've loved playing with him.

Once, there was a hole in the ground. I was terrified but Boby wanted to go in. I said no but he went in anyway. I cried until dawn. Suddenly, it went quiet. It was Boby. I ran to him. I asked what was it like down there.

He said, "Fun! Come and see for yourself!"

I went through the hole. It was beautiful down there. I loved it there.

Bella Fleischer (9)

Ashfield Junior School, Bushey

My Second Amazing Find And My Third Amazing Find

Dear Diary,

I was walking on the beach, pondering my last discovery when I found another find! It was kind of like my last one but it had a much smaller eye. I called the four quarrymen to help me carry it. I took it back to my humble abode and got my mining tools. I chipped at it.

A couple of years later, I found another one. It was more bird-like than a sea creature. I took it back and mined it with the chisel patiently. Once that was done I didn't find any more discoveries.

Charlie Jacobs (10)
Ashfield Junior School, Bushey

Dream

Dear Diary,

Yesterday was the best day of my life. It all started at a football training club in London. It was a normal Friday until I went to training. What I didn't know was that there was a football scout looking for people to play for Arsenal. They called me over and said I was the right person for Arsenal. I was so excited and was just frozen on the spot.

The next day it was so hot but the only thing on my mind was that I had got scouted for Arsenal. I was so happy.

Ella Holden (9)

Ashfield Junior School, Bushey

My Discoveries

Dear Diary,

I was on the beach when I saw something big. It was a huge skull. I chipped and chipped until it was complete. I was astonished when I saw it. There was a man who came over to buy it. I got a friend of mine to come and she was amazed when she saw it. Before he bought it, I named it the ichthyosaur and I got £45 and five shillings. Everyone saw it when they came to my shop. I made money, lots of it. I became the greatest female, famous, fantastic fossil hunter.

Leo Soteriou (9)

Ashfield Junior School, Bushey

A Diary Account Of The Life Of Mary Anning

Dear Diary,
Me and my beloved father went fossil hunting in Lyme Regis when suddenly, he fell off a very steep cliff. I was terrified of what had happened and I was panicking. He was in the hospital for nine months. Then he unfortunately died. I was devastated and I lost hope. But I found a lovely and friendly dog so I carried on fossil hunting with my new friend. Life is hard now Father is not around but I will never forget the memories I made with him.
From Mary Anning.

Antonia Rai (10)
Ashfield Junior School, Bushey

Dear Diary

Dear Diary,

Me and Mason were playing a game called 'It'. We had lots of fun. We went home and ate snacks and we watched a movie called Mario. Then we fell asleep.

The next morning, we went into a pool and we splashed water as a shooter. Then we brought pizza, chips and sweets. Later we ate it all.

Then we explored the city. We saw a pool and a bus, a sweet shop and a teddy bear shop. We saw a chip shop and we bought some chips and fish and we ate it all.

Kyle Tugwood (8)

Ashfield Junior School, Bushey

My Amazing Discoveries

Dear Diary,
Today, I discovered an ichthyosaur. It was so towering. It will glance back in time to discover it. I was on the beach and I found a curiosity. I chipped my first pieces of built-up mud. I found out it was an ichthyosaur. I thought it would take me fifty years to get the whole thing down. It is so amazing just to observe right now. I can only think of it. I am probably going to get lots of visits. I will happily get some money from it.

Jessica Blowers (9)
Ashfield Junior School, Bushey

Khloe And Poppy Met Each Other At Swimming

Dear Diary,

Some time ago, I was four months old. I went swimming with my mum. We saw a girl called Khloe. We decided to ask her if we could be her friend. After we had asked her she said yes. Obviously, her mum was there too.

The next time I saw her was when we were two and one. When we got there, Khloe was a couple of minutes late but we still had fun. Sometime after, we started nursery but by the time we had got to year two I had to leave.

Poppy (9)

Ashfield Junior School, Bushey

A Diary Account Of The Life Of Mary Anning

Dear Diary,
Today I remembered how I felt when I found the first plesiosaur on Earth. I found it in Lyme Regis and I felt a feeling. A feeling I can't describe or say in words. It was a proud, happy and sad feeling. I was happy since it helped our family a lot. I was also sad because my father wasn't with me when I found it. But I know wherever he is, he is proud of me.
Mary Anning.

Taiki Muranaka (10)
Ashfield Junior School, Bushey

A Diary Account Of The Life Of Mary Anning

Dear Diary,

A few days ago, when my kind father was fossil hunting, he was right on the peak of a cliff. But he accidentally tripped and fell off the huge cliff.

My father had died on a huge cliff on the very peak by falling off it. I felt really sad that my great father had died. I could never imagine him dying. I always wish that he would come back.

From Mary Anning.

Logan Little (9)

Ashfield Junior School, Bushey

A Diary Account Of The Life Of Mary Anning

Dear Diary,

I would have written yesterday but my father died. After he died all my thoughts and emotions came to me. I was angry because everything bad happens to me. I am getting bullied, people calling me names and my father has just died. Sometimes I think I was not meant to come into this world. Now it is just me and my little annoying brother. From Mary.

Louis De La Cour (9)

Ashfield Junior School, Bushey

The Incredible Diary Of Bella Dog

Dear Diary,

I was on a walk. By the way, my name is Bella Dog. Oh, let's get back to the diary. I was on a walk and I was in a wood when I got lost. I walked for a while until I saw a peculiar-looking flower. I picked it up... when everything turned magical. Then along came my cat brother.

"What are you doing here?" I asked.

"I was..."

"*Ruff ruff!* Get out of here."

"Okay, okay, geez, stop being so *angry!*"

"Okay, but *go.*"

Such a dumb cat. I woke up. I couldn't believe I was *dreaming!*

Darcey Tuer (9)

Barnard Castle Preparatory School, Barnard Castle

Superheroes In The Supermarket

Dear Diary,
You won't believe this... I was shopping with Mum when... *Bam!* Superman came flying into the shop, breaking everything in his path. Coming in fast behind him through the smashed window was Lex Luthor. He picked Superman up and... *Wham!* Superman smashed off the shop walls. He screamed in pain as Lex Luthor threw him across the store. As Lex charged his final attack, Batman came flying down and threw batarangs at Lex. Superman tackled Lex, slamming them both through a wall. Batman came swooping in, trapping Lex with a net, and then the police took Lex away!

Alexander Carr (10)

Barnard Castle Preparatory School, Barnard Castle

Algae's Diary

Dear Diary,

It was my first day at my brand-new school, I was quite nervous. I didn't know anyone and I knew a lot of people at my old school. I'm different in a way. I've come from outer space! I've been sent by my mother and father. So far I've had some interesting lessons but there's one human who definitely doesn't like me. Then it was lunch. Things were different than normal, but I had fish and chips. After, it was home time, it was a painful day. I don't want to come back to this horrible, horrible place.

Edith Smart (9)
Barnard Castle Preparatory School, Barnard Castle

The Diary Of Jammy Sammy The Incredible Hero

Dear Diary,

Yesterday I flew to the famous New York City. But, while I was relaxing with Mystery Man and Banana Barnaby, an evil titan wandered out of a portal in the clouds. Epic! But it wasn't epic for long. He started shooting sound beams out of his massive hands. They were like seven metres tall. Anyway, that's beside the point. We all leapt into battle and tried to defeat him. I was trembling in fear. He got so close that I thought it was all over; it wasn't. Little did he know, I'm resilient and I never give up...

Barnaby Tiplady (10)

Barnard Castle Preparatory School, Barnard Castle

Bat Monkey

Dear Diary,

Yesterday was great, there was sun in Monknum City. Then there was a podcast on the radio. It said the Joker Monkey was on the loose. I sprang into action and went to the last place he was spotted. I found him in a dark alleyway and I said, "Let's do this."

He said, "Go on, come at me!"

So we started to brawl. I threw a batarang and it exploded.

He was tired and I said, "I can do this all day."

He was on the ground so I got him to go to jail.

Andrew Barker (10)

Barnard Castle Preparatory School, Barnard Castle

The Incredible Diary Of A New World

One day there was a boy called Wonder. He dreamed of going to space, he loved space and was so interested in it. So he spent years and years building a rocket and today was the day he tried it. Wonder was very clever and knew what he was doing, but still, this could go wrong. He tried it and so he went to pack his bag and waved goodbye. Off he went, and just two hours later he'd landed. What an amazing discovery he'd made. He was so pleased and wanted to stay. He'd always remember this special day.

Acer Tarn (9)

Barnard Castle Preparatory School, Barnard Castle

The Unfortunate Wombat

I am a wombat. I sleep most of the day. My usual routine is sleep, sleep, lunch (grass), sleep, dig, tea (grass) and sleep. You should think my life is pretty boring, and you are right, until yesterday. I got hit by a broom, stung by bees, surely my day could not get any worse. But it got much worse. After lunch, it started raining. My burrow filled up with water so I had to sleep in a dog kennel. But today I got an ice cream with carrot and had the best day ever. My burrow is dry, yay!

Matilda Small (8)
Barnard Castle Preparatory School, Barnard Castle

The Incredible Diary Of Mr Krabs

Dear Diary,
Last night I was dreaming about all my *money* and me being rich. I was also dreaming about losing *all* my money. The next day, when I woke up, I was on the street and I lost *all my money*, it was just like my dream! I worked a long and hard day. I found a place to sleep, next to a bin, but when I woke up, I was in a palace and I had a butler and I had a *vault* with one *million* pounds in it!
See you next time Diary, bye-bye.

Sienna Barras (9)
Barnard Castle Preparatory School, Barnard Castle

The Diary Of Daffy

Today was amazing, I was planted in a strange place by a giant called Dave. He seemed nice but soon it all went black, and that's when it started! I woke up that morning, I saw something brown and white coming up to me. It started to sniff me and then it weed on me! It was cold like ice. Everyone looked at my friend but not me, just because I was different. I saw a lot of giants that day, but just before I was going to sleep, a fast giant passed me and knocked me over!

Jessica Read (10)
Barnard Castle Preparatory School, Barnard Castle

I Love Kittens

I love kittens so very much. They are so cute and cuddly and so soft, they are so, so everything that kittens are! Myself, I have no kittens, not one at all, I really, really want one. The next day, guess what my mom and I did? We went to... a phone shop. It was absolutely boring! On the way back, I made my mom pull over at the side of the road because I needed a wee, but guess what? I nearly weed on a homeless kitten. I took the kitten off the side of the road...

Violet Ellis (7)

Barnard Castle Preparatory School, Barnard Castle

Bob's Adventure

When Bob arrived, he found an igloo. He found people in the igloo. The people had some ice axes. They went to climb with the ice axes. They went climbing and a bit of ice fell, so they went back to the igloo. They found a baby penguin looking for its mum and it was hungry, so they fed it some fish. The baby penguin found his mum. Bob and Joe had a submarine and they got into it and went back home.

Fenn Reid (7)
Barnard Castle Preparatory School, Barnard Castle

Gold

One day in Lego City, a new car arrived. The car was gold. It parked in a gold house. A gold person went into the house. Everything was gold. The person's name was Goldy. The next day it rained and he could not go outside because his gold would drop off and he would die! The next day, he did a race, it was a marathon. He was in first place but it was very close. He won a trophy!

Bertie Trevor (6)
Barnard Castle Preparatory School, Barnard Castle

The Magical, Mysterious Cosmic Portal

Dear Diary,

Today something ridiculous happened as soon as I left school. There was an oval shape with an inky exterior and a navy interior. I stared at it for a minute until I realised it was an intergalactic portal which led to space. I felt over the moon until I saw a creepy monster which had a red body and it looked like he'd had a haircut for a century. The monster glared at me so I sprinted out of the strange place. I told my friends all about my short and petrifying voyage. Bye for now!

Keshigan Ragumaran (9)

Bentley St Paul's CE (VA) Primary School, Bentley

Where Is She?

Dear Diary,

A fortnight ago my friend Lily and I were walking home when Lily was dragged abruptly into a nearby bush. I went to go find her when I fell down a hole. Then I found myself in a forest. Suddenly, I saw her but at that moment a mysterious serrated pine needle pierced her neck. I then woke up. I thought it was a dream. Later I was at her funeral. Was it a coincidence? As I went to lay a flower on her body I saw a pine needle in her neck. "It couldn't be!" I gasped.

Olivia Taiwo Bajomo (9)

Bentley St Paul's CE (VA) Primary School, Bentley

The Boy And The Flower

It was a sunny day, the sun was as bright as the moon shining at night when suddenly a flower was blocking my beautiful sunlight! I wanted to play football, but I was determined to play the thing I loved most. I asked Mum, "Why is this ugly, beastly flower out there?" She said nothing so I asked Dad if I could use his chainsaw. He said yes so I went over to that ugly flower and chopped it down! Now I could play football! I invited my friends and we had a lot of fun! I was very happy.

Beau Bucknall (11)

Bentley St Paul's CE (VA) Primary School, Bentley

The Brain Suction

Dear Diary,

I forgot to write last night but a lot happened today so let me tell you... I woke up this morning in a bed but not my bed and I was strapped. There was a hat-like item on my head, it was sucking out everything - my memory, my words. I struggled and struggled and finally broke free. I started to search around for an exit! There in the corner, there was a trapdoor. There were five seconds left on the bomb. It opened and I jumped out. I was free! I'll never come back...

Elisa Chambrier (10)

Bentley St Paul's CE (VA) Primary School, Bentley

Dear Diary, Two Sky Night

Off I go, take a deep breath, and fly! I was jumping off the world's biggest mountain ever seen for the first time- *Knock, knock.*

"Mum?"

"Can you please stop pretending you're flying and stop jumping on your bed?"

"But none of this would have happened if you walked in, anyway I told you not to come in."

"Huh, and take those wings off!"

"But I superglued them on..."

"Oh yeah?"

"I superglued them on!"

"What?"

"Mum, I'm not kidding, help me! Help me!"

"I can't, it's- it's stuck!"

And that was the end. They were stuck.

Prudence Tombs (8)
Berkeley Primary School, Berkeley

Into The Future

Dear Diary,
I woke up in this weird dimension. There were people with more than two eyes, some people were robots and some were aliens. There were animals mixed together called gookos. The most dangerous one was a massive spider that had venom like a venomous snake. The buildings were on fire, people laughing. Everyone was crazy, no one was helping me. There was no escape from this nightmare. Then a man came to me and said, "Hey, I know a way. Go in this escape room and find a way out."
I went in and realised I was stuck.

William Tremlett (10)

Blaise Primary & Nursery School, Henbury

The Crash

Dear Diary,

Today something bad happened in Timmy Station when I and Jim moved trains. A bit later we derailed and slid down a mountain. We were crashing. I jumped out and Jim stayed in then the train exploded. I was seriously hurt and many people died. Police were called. I went to hospital but soon I was healthy again. I went back to driving trains and I was more careful. It was weird but everything was okay after that. This is being written during my lunch, also a mean passenger complained a lot.

Jamal Rivers (10)

Blaise Primary & Nursery School, Henbury

Harriled The Stick

Dear Diary,
A stick was lonely and nobody cared about him. The only thing they did was get the stick and threw it around. I am the stick that nobody cared about and everybody threw me to dogs and the dog chewed me and left me on the floor at the dark, cold park.

Then one day, I thought to run away so I packed and started walking but then a girl came so I lay still. She picked me up and said, "I like you!" so she gave me a name, Harriled, and then she took me home.

Angelina Naijil (10)
Blaise Primary & Nursery School, Henbury

The Improvement Of A Young Hero

Dear Diary,

I woke up from my coma today and suddenly felt like I had to seek revenge. I could remember exactly what happened against Shigaraki.

The first thing I remember, everyone was talking about my quirk. The next thing, I was fighting him. I was winning, until I froze completely.

Shigarki shot spikes from his fingers and I was going to die. Bakugo jumped in front of me and he was injured badly. That's when I lost it.

I was invincible, no one could stop me now. My eyes were bright green. I bit through the spikes. Goodbye.

Ava Evans (11)

Brockholes Wood ASC, Preston

The Last Day Of The World

Dear Diary,

Today is my birthday and the last day of the world. So first, I met my best friend Sophia and we ate a gallon of ice cream.

Later in a jet rocket, we flew to the sun and met a snowman! Lastly, me and Sophia got abducted into heaven. In heaven, we flew around castles and clouds for eternity.

Today was magnificent! I felt so cheerful today but upset because it was the last day of the world. At the end of the day, me and Sophia sat on clouds, dreaming of what amazing adventures we will have!

Ruqaya Al-Saati (10)

Brockholes Wood ASC, Preston

The School Day

Yesterday, I had the most enthusiastic day of my life. So we were at school, then there was a fire alarm. So we all ran outside. After the register, we all ran back inside to go get the football.

Then I kicked the football over the fence, so we went to go and get it. When we arrived at the place where the football landed, we saw someone taking a load of all our balls and they ran away with our balls!

We were shocked. We followed him but he ended up at Domino's and it was Mr Beast!

Karrar Al-Saati (8)
Brockholes Wood ASC, Preston

The Big Day

Dear Diary,

My mom had been keeping a secret for a week. She wouldn't give me or my sister a clue, but we did know it was in London.

My sister looked up coming things in London and saw USA vs England, it was right. We left on Thursday. When we got there, we got ready and went.

We got a drink and went in. When it ended, England won 2-1.

When that ended, I went home and when I got back, I played on my PS4 and chilled up until school started again.

Jake Evans (9)

Brockholes Wood ASC, Preston

The Disappearing Horses

Dear Diary,

Today was the most intense and scariest day I have ever had! Emily and I were having a sleepover and decided to have a ride with our ponies. While I was helping Emily tack up her pony, Rosy, we heard a thud. We turned back to see Star's door open and her stall empty! "Jack!" I called, annoyed at my brother, who was at a club. *What!* I thought, puzzled. We went back to see people who were trying to steal Rosy! We tackled them heroically and led them out, taking Rosy and Star back to the barn.

Megu Mizuno (11)

Buxlow Preparatory School, Wembley

CR7

CR7 went in an interview and disrespected United owners and managers. He said the owners were awful and CR7 is currently the lead of goals with eight hundred and twenty-nine and has a celebration where he jumps in the air and says Siu, karma slides and takes his T-shirt off. He has played for United, Real Madrid, Sporting, Juventus and Al-Nassr. He made a skill called Ronaldo chop, scores hat-tricks, doesn't like Diego Simeone and has another celebration where he holds his chest and that's when he scores his hundredth club goal. He is the greatest of all.

Dillon Bradbury (10)

Chorlton Park Primary School, Chorlton

A Strange World

The story starts with me waking up at 8:00, getting ready for another day at school. At around 8:45, we set off to school, not noticing that the neighbour's cat was acting unusually unusual. At school, our maths teacher, Miss Jhonson, the oldest teacher, had a daughter who had a daughter that was in the school. Miss Jhonson's daughter was turning twenty-five this year. When I was daydreaming in maths class, I saw the neighbour's cat aggressively scratching the pipe as if it was a scratching post. Moments later, an army of cats had come...

Zayan Chowdhury (10)
Chorlton Park Primary School, Chorlton

Day Of A Football

Dear Diary,

Today started with me sitting (like usual) next to my round friends when some gloved hands picked me up out of the basket. I was thrown into a trolley and then the following things were dumped on top of me: a whistle, a red card, a yellow card, a football kit, some football boots and a hat. I was then wheeled out of my shop and onto the street. Soon I was thrown onto the grass and kicked around. It felt like hours before I was booted into a net and left covered in black and blue bruises.

William Harvest (10)

Chorlton Park Primary School, Chorlton

A Really Bad Day

Dear Diary,

Yesterday was so painful. I kept getting hit on the bum with weird sticks with a hook on the end, repeatedly, like I was an unwanted rat on the floor or something.

At one point, I was sleeping in a box with my siblings then, next, I was being flicked into a big metal box with a person inside with a protective foam uniform on, acting like they were going to get seriously injured.

But what about me? I'm the one with a weird stick on my bum and children running around shouting, "Pass here!"

Elodie Milward (11)
Christ Church Academy, Stone

The Hurt Boy

Dear Diary,

Me and my friend were playing on the playground when something horrible happened - someone fell over! They were crying because they slipped on the ice, it was an icy day.

I felt really bad, so I went to help him up, but he didn't want my help. I could tell he was in pain, so I asked him, "Are you okay?"

He just said, "Go away!" Then a teacher helped him up.

That's why I never want to play on ice again! I was scared from then. I always want to help people now.

Alyssa-May Crowther (11)

Christ Church Academy, Stone

The Ultimate Game

Dear Diary,

Today, I was sitting on the playing board. Here came the attack! It was by the other team's queen. But I'm the vital piece - I'm the king, the best piece on the board! If I get taken, then my whole squad loses.

It is a challenging game to play. Little moves mean so much! But my team haven't lost a game yet. It gives us hope to win against the best team.

It is agonising to wait for it to finish but, finally, it was over. My team won and I didn't have to move a square.

Harry Norwood (10)

Christ Church Academy, Stone

The Day My Suitcase Glowed

Dear Diary,

Yesterday, I was packing my suitcase, getting ready for my holiday. I went to the toilet, but something caught my eye - my suitcase was glowing!

My instincts said for me to not look, but I did and I saw a tunnel. So, without a second, I jumped in.

I can't even explain the place it took me to. There were rainbows, the colours were as bright as the sun. And there were dolphins. Also, there was a beach with crabs that delivered your food and drinks. Oh, it was amazing.

Lilly-May Dee (10)

Christ Church Academy, Stone

Under Attack

Dear Diary,

My school was under attack by the military because someone at the school had a knife. So we were under attack. They came in as a group so the school was like, ahh!

They kicked the maths door down. I was in the room next to the maths room, so I stood up and ran out, all the way to the science lab because it has all the types of technology.

But I didn't use them, I just dropped them and ran out of the fire exit. I saw a bush and climbed through and ran out.

Charlie Woodall (11)

Christ Church Academy, Stone

Dog Man

Dear Diary,

Today, I woke up to an alarm. Then I went to fight crime with my friends. We were fighting a huge robot with our enemy who made a clone of himself, but he gave him to us.

I am the leader of the team and I'm a police animal with a human body. They're making a movie about me.

We went to fight the robot and he kicked 80-HD to another country. Then his charge went to 100%. Then 80-HD came flying as fast as light and destroyed the robot in a second.

Oliver Humphries (10)

Christ Church Academy, Stone

Marm-Tastic

Dear Diary,

Today was spread day AKA the worst day ever. I was lying in my jar when the lid opened and the light almost blinded me. I felt scared as a sharp blade was lowered into my home and scraped me up.

The blade was cold and put me on some warm bread. The bread was put on a plate, as the humans call them, and before I knew it - I had been eaten!

I was trapped in a mouth and, soon enough, I was surfing down the throat on some bread. It was magnificent.

Connor O'leary (11)

Christ Church Academy, Stone

So We Brought Them Home

Dear Diary,
Today was wonderful. We were going to pick up a dog from a farm. We finally got there and there were three dogs, one boy and two girls. The girl was shy but the boy wasn't, so we picked the boy. We drove off. All of a sudden, we came across a foal on the road. We picked him up and took him. Next, we saw a tiger! So we brought him too. Then we saw a herd of animals so we brought them home.
That's how we started our zoo! It was exciting.

Holly McPherson (11)
Christ Church Academy, Stone

My Spanish Holiday

Dear Diary,

I went on holiday to Spain and I am going to write about it. So, on day one, I spent most of the day in the pool and it was really good. I had salad and pudding.

We did that for a few days and then we went to the beach. We were wave jumping.

In the evening, we did the entertainment from 7 'til 11. It was mainly karaoke and disco. The disco was cool. After that, we did the conga and played pool, also arcade games. And that's my diary.

Harry Pearsall (11)

Christ Church Academy, Stone

Leo Messi And The Ghost Stadium

Dear Diary,
I got out of bed and went for a walk. On the walk, I saw a stadium. It was covered in leaves all around it, which made me think it was haunted.

I was about to go in, but I forgot that I needed a ticket. No one was in the ticket office. I went in and opened the doors. Now that I'd opened them, I could go in.

When I got in, I thought of playing football, which I did. But I heard ghosts. Now I thought it was a ghost stadium. I quickly ran.

Harvey Rowson (10)
Christ Church Academy, Stone

Vampire Tragedy

Dear Diary,

Today was insane! My bestie said that a strange creature was at her door. How do I know? They had video proof!

Once I saw the footage, I was stunned. A real-life pixie had knocked at her door at 3am! I was surprised.

When she told me, I ran home and informed Mum. She didn't believe me at first, but as I showed her the footage she freaked out.

Day 2,

I just realised my best friend is a vampire!

Jessica Allinson (9)

Christ Church Academy, Stone

A Day At The Museum

My birthday treat was to visit the British Museum! I was very excited to see the Rosetta Stone face-to-face. The stone was in front of me. I reached out to touch the rough surface. The room started spinning and I wasn't in the museum. I blinked twice and saw a gigantic figure with a white beard holding a magnificent thunderbolt! I couldn't believe where I was! It was ancient Greece and I was on Mount Olympus. The gods, Ares, Zeus and Poseidon were arguing. All of a sudden, they turned to look at me... *Help!* I'm stuck in Greece!

Ayyub Ansari (8)

Cranbrook Primary School, Ilford

My Adventure

Dear Diary,

This is a story about my adventure.

Once, I went to go get my mum some chicken nuggets and on the way, a fairy came up to me and said, "Little girl, do you want some speed?" I said yes since it was a long walk.

As soon as the fairy finished the spell, I was amazingly fast! Once I had finally got the chicken nuggets, I saw the same fairy again and she asked if I got there quickly. "Yes, I did!" I replied. "I'm also very tired."

I got home and gave Mum the chicken nuggets.

Inaya Haque (9)

Cranbrook Primary School, Ilford

The Seaside

One evening, my family decided to go visit the beach. I was very excited. We went on a train to reach our destination. We built many sandcastles. My dad bought ice cream for us. Then we went in the sea to have a little swim. From the seashore, we went on all the rides. I sat on all the rides for my age. My favourite ride was the roller coaster. The scariest ride was Rage.

After that, we got cotton candy. I loved it, it was the best! We finished our day with hot chocolate. It was an unforgettable day.

Yusuf Shaikh (8)

Cranbrook Primary School, Ilford

The Best Strike Day!

Dear Diary,

On Thursday, it was teachers' strike day. I was so joyful because I was going to my friend's birthday! I bought the best Lego that he would be flabbergasted by. I was cheerful. I wore my new clothes. As quick as a flash, I ran downstairs and got in the car. By the time I arrived, they were cutting the cake.

Later, I joined in and sang the happy birthday song. Then I played football. Then I had to go home, but it was worth it because I had so much fun, which is crazy!

Ismaeel Choudhry (9)

Cranbrook Primary School, Ilford

Outer Space

One day, I decided to go to space because I am an astronaut and the other astronauts were going. So we went to space and I decided to go on a spacewalk. So I told the other astronauts. I put my tethering cord on and went for a spacewalk. Suddenly, the tethering cord broke. I tried calling for help, but no one heard.

After a while, they realised I was gone. So they came to rescue me. Luckily, they came back in time. We went back to the rocket and went back to Earth. I'd never go back.

Amelia Ahmed (9)

Cranbrook Primary School, Ilford

My Rainforest Adventure

Dear Diary,

Once in a dark, mysterious forest, I woke up confused about where I was. I walked around and searched my surroundings. I was in the Amazon Rainforest! No way! *How did I get here?*
Huh? What was that? *Boom!*

Haoyu Yang (9)

Cranbrook Primary School, Ilford

Bulgaria

Dear Diary,

Yesterday was a great day! I finally went on a plane since 2017 and it was so so fun! I came all the way to Bulgaria to see my family but it is hot, like scorching hot.

Firstly, I went to the capital city of Bulgaria - Sofia. Then I visited the grand Alexander Nevsky church. After that, I went to a crystal shop, my absolute favourite thing in the entire world!

After that, I went home and ate a rather appetising spaghetti that I helped my uncle make. Later on, I watched some Netflix and went to bed.

Simona Yordanova (11)

Dothill Primary School, Wellington

The School Is Floating!

Dear Diary,

I went to school and I saw everything off the ground. When I got inside, everything was floating. Paintbrushes and palettes were flying everywhere. Then it all fell and started flying everywhere again. We did some work on the floor because the chairs were floating. Then we went outside to play and everything was floating outside as well.

When we came back in, we all tried to figure out why everything was floating. There was a switch to turn it off and it was a normal day again.

Kaylyn Marshall (11)

Drummore Primary School, Stranraer

Dear Diary

Dear Diary,
Today was the craziest day ever! First, I woke up really tired but my mum shouted at me, "Go downstairs, you'll be late for work!" I did what she said. As I got there she made me honey waffles and they were delicious! I went outside the hive to find some nectar and pollen. I found a beautiful purple flower with lots of pollen but a little bit of nectar. I was furious but I heard footsteps getting louder and closer so I hid behind the beautiful purple flower. I realised it was a spider! I cowered...

Tymon (8)

Gardners Lane Primary School, Cheltenham

The Diary Of Brenda The Bee

Dear Diary,

Today, as usual, I went out to collect nectar and I flew to a beautiful rose, a human swatted me and I was terrified so I flew to the field to a beautiful daffodil instead! I sucked up the nectar and flew away to another flower. I realised a butterfly was following me! I turned around to the butterfly but it flew away. I felt confused - was the butterfly stalking me or trying to be my friend? I was going back to the hive to make some honey when I was at the hive and started working tiredly!

Nurgul Aslan (9)

Gardners Lane Primary School, Cheltenham

The Private Diary Of Belinda The Bee

Dear Diary,

Today I went to the zoo. I saw bears, lions, alligators - I also saw bees! I was angry! I tried to break the glass and a bee said, "We like it here." I saw humans in there and asked why they were there - they said they were beekeepers, that's what they called themselves. I didn't like them in their funny suits. I went to the park and drank some nectar. I got some pollen to bring to the hive. I gave it to the pollen collectors and went home to go to sleep.

Tommy Baron (8)

Gardners Lane Primary School, Cheltenham

Dear Diary

Dear Diary,

I jumped out of the comfortable bed and did the waggle dance with my brother. My sister and I then brushed our teeth. We all ate the wonderful honey pancakes. I went outside to collect the beautiful flowers. I went to the hive with the pollen. My brother and I then danced with the other bees in the hive. My sister and I then had a honey sandwich. I went to the amazing honey work. I came back and tiredly ate the golden cake. I went to the living room and sat down.

Garvit Nagpal (8)

Gardners Lane Primary School, Cheltenham

The Incredible Diary Of Bella The Bee!

Dear Diary,
Yesterday I had the best day! I went outside to visit my fifteen hundred flowers and I met a wasp. He said his name was Wonka the Wasp, I said mine was Bella the Bee. We became good friends. I was on my last flower so after I collected some nectar, I went into the park with Wonka. We had such fun! I went home after saying bye to Wonka. I told my Mum all about it - I was ecstatic! Then today I saw Wonka again, I was glad. We became best friends - yay! Best days ever!

Maame Boateng-Bandoh (9)
Gardners Lane Primary School, Cheltenham

The Amazing Diary Of Daisy The Bee

Dear Diary,

I had the most amazing day! First I got ready and had honey for breakfast, then the most exciting part - I went out of the hive! I buzzed to a beautiful-smelling flower and started to collect nectar from it. Then I saw some more flowers in a house and I went inside. I tried to get nectar from them but then I found out they were fake! Next I went out of the house and started seeing more fabulous flowers. I buzzed to get them then I went back to the hive. What a day!

Sophia White (9)

Gardners Lane Primary School, Cheltenham

A Bee's Diary

Dear Diary,
Today was a nice day. First I went to meet my friend Volt, then I went to continue to help Queen Bee lay eggs. After that I asked Queen if I could go out but she said "No!" I was getting bored so I sneaked out of the hive. When I got out, everywhere looked so beautiful. I buzzed around for some time and then found a garden. When I went over the fence, I saw Volt and I think he saw me. I entered the garden, saw a gardener and then I collected the pollen.

Adeife Aribisala (8)
Gardners Lane Primary School, Cheltenham

The Troubles Of A Bee

Dear Diary,
Today was my best day ever because I went out for my sweet delicious honey. I went out and saw the beautiful colours but I felt one gone and that was like all my life! Then a person left a kite then a clown was juggling some balls really high. After that it hit me and I went down. Then people were playing football. I got knocked out. One bee saw me knocked out and he went back to the hive and told the others. They all came and the people were scared and ran away!

Kochyar Garib (9)
Gardners Lane Primary School, Cheltenham

Dear Diary

I woke up and got out of my yellow bed. For breakfast, I ate hot honey for my food and nectar for my drink. I jumped out of the hive and flew around the beautiful world. My work is to collect pollen. After my break I made honey. It is hard work. After work, I flew home. It was a beautiful world and I was happy. When it was raining I was cross because I got wet.

I went home for dinner. I ate nectar and pollen for dinner.

Jaydon Finn (8)

Gardners Lane Primary School, Cheltenham

The Diary Of A Bee

Dear Diary,

Today was a good day because we were finding flowers and then we went back to the hive. We were making honey and the Queen was laying eggs. She kept laying eggs so we had to go and get more honey and get all the pollen. It was boring and getting even more boring until we got to the last flower. It was finally done - yay! I had got everything I needed so I could go back to the hive to make more honey.

Tyler O'Neill (9)

Gardners Lane Primary School, Cheltenham

Dear Diary

I woke up and did the waggle dance. I went downstairs and ate sugary pancakes. I got nectar from flowers and went back and turned it into honey for the Queen Bee. I felt happy with myself but it was raining. I went under a leaf so my wings didn't get wet. My mum said, "You are going to be late for work!" but I was so tired I couldn't move. I just ate more golden sugary pancakes.

Holly Borley (8)
Gardners Lane Primary School, Cheltenham

Dear Diary

Dear Diary,

I had a bad dream and I was playing with my friends Bella and Andrea when Bella broke my expensive locket. My mum woke me up and I told the dream to my mum but then I had golden, sticky honey pancakes.

David Velescu (8)

Gardners Lane Primary School, Cheltenham

Everton Versus Manchester United

Once I was walking in town and I saw a massive, huge stadium. It was Everton versus Manchester United. It was a really interesting game. It was 1-1 at overtime at half-time and Everton had a lot of chances. There were thirty minutes left of the game. Calvert-Lewin went to the football and smacked it top bins. He scored. Such an amazing top bins. Everton was happy but Manchester United was very emotional and sad, but it still was not over yet. Man United still had a chance. But there was one minute left of the game. Everton Town won.

Louie Garner (8)
Gayton CE Primary School, Gayton

An Exciting Day

Dear Diary,

Today I had a fun day. Holly and Daisy Trower came to our house to play. Two of us jumped on the trampoline and the other two played badminton. We then played a horror game in reality. Later, we watched a movie together called 'We Can Be Heroes'. Afterwards, we played 'break in reality'. Finally, Daisy and Holly Trower had to go home. On the way back, we picked up Daddy from the haircutters.

Chloe To (7)

Gayton CE Primary School, Gayton

The Diary Of The Hungry Wolf

Dear Diary,

It is early in the morning and I can't wait to tell you about my day.

Yesterday I went on a walk in the woods and I met a little girl. I felt hungry. I pretended to be the little girl's grandma but the woodcutter came to save her.

Finally, I went home hungry.

Darcy Taylor (7)

Greatstone Primary School, Greatstone

The Hairy Wolf

It's 2am and I'm writing my diary.
I went for a walk and I met a little girl in the woods. I went to her grandma's house but a woodcutter came and hit me on the head so I went home hungry.

Henry-Joe Nightingale (6)

Greatstone Primary School, Greatstone

Bahrain's New Year's Eve

Dear Diary,

On New Year's Eve (31.12.22) I felt really excited because soon was 2023. My uncle, mum and little sister were also excited. I was in Bahrain Bay. Bahrain is an island in the Persian Gulf.

After around twenty minutes it was finally New Year's Day and there were huge, mind-capturing, unbelievable fireworks exploding in the midnight sky. The crowds of excited, euphoric people had joy in their hearts while the fireworks were coming and going constantly, banging and exploding loudly. After it all finished people rushed to their cars to get through traffic. What an amazing event!

Hashim Zeeshan Zulfeqar (9)

Greenhill Primary School, Bury

RIP Baby Khaleel

Mum was expecting a baby. When she went to the first scan the doctors showed the baby scan to Mum and Dad. Mum's tummy was growing slowly bigger. Mum and Dad found out the baby was a boy, which made me happy because I always wanted a brother.

My baby brother was not well. Then my dad told me that the baby was really ill. Baby Khaleel died two months before he was meant to be born. I cried a lot.

Baby Khaleel is buried in the cemetery near my house. We believe Khaleel is waiting for us in Heaven.

Khadijah Hussain (9)

Greenhill Primary School, Bury

Diary Of An Embarrassed Kid

Dear Diary,
Today I was at school and my grandparents decided to come visit. They screamed across the playground, "Don't walk with food in your mouth, Elfi!" And to be honest, I felt so embarrassed. But that's only one part of my story.
Later we were coming out from school, I was the last one out as usual. When I saw them they were literally leaning over the ramp to pick me up. I tried to get them to move so other people could get out but they wouldn't budge.

Elfi Jones (8)
Greenhill Primary School, Bury

Ella, Hope And The Mystery

One day, two girls called Ella and Hope were getting ready for bed when all of a sudden they heard a noise. It was scary. It sounded like a voice, but it didn't sound like anyone's voice in the house. They didn't think anything of it so went off to bed. It was morning now and the girls had already gotten ready for school. They were on their way to school when they found a wand. Ella picked it up and showed Hope. They both waved the wand, it turned the school into a castle. "Wow, how magical!" they gasped.

Jessica Wilson (9)
Halfway Primary School, Llanelli

The Ballerina

There was a girl called Lexi and she was a ballerina. She had a competition against other girls and she wanted to win, so she practised every day and her friends were Riley and Evan.

The next day it was the competition. She was so nervous to perform, then she had to go up. She was doing well but then she fell and she burst out crying, but then she felt confident to go on stage and perform. She was still scared to perform but she did very well and because of that, she won. Lexi was happy now.

Aathana Sanjeevan (9)

Halfway Primary School, Llanelli

Ms Pencil And Her 'Don't Know What To Do Right Now' Owner

Dear Diary,

This is a day in the life of Ms Pencil and her owner... Hazel. Hello dear humans, I am here to tell you about my petrifying... problem! Now as a human, in your human brain, you're probably thinking, *what, Ms Pencil, has your lead snapped?* No silly, my problem is way worse than that. My problem is due to being so short because of sharpening! My owner is going to be using my worst, and yes I mean worst enemy as her new pencil! That is way worse than my pencil lead snapping isn't it?!

Evelyn Burton (10)

Hatchell Wood Primary Academy, Bessacarr

Hogwarts Legacy

Dear Diary,
I got a letter from an owl but my mean brother, Bob, took it before I could get it. Once I got my hands on it, I read it. It said: 'Invitation from Hogwarts School of Witchcraft and Wizardry."
Last month, I set off to get a wand, an owl and the firebolt with the money Mum gave me. Last week, I became a Gryffindor and I made two new friends, Tom and Sarah. I set a new record for the fastest time to become a seeker, beating my dad, Harry Potter, and becoming the strongest wizard ever.

Leo Baxter (11)

Highfields Primary Academy, Highfields

Day In The Life Of Harvey Jake!

Dear Diary,

Today I went to the park. I went on the swing but I fell off. Me and my friend, Bob, started laughing. We then went to play football. I won. Yes! I felt hungry. Bob felt hungry.

"I want McDonald's," said Bob.

We went to McDonald's on our bicycles. I had a Happy Meal and so did Bob. Then we went home and went on the Xbox. Then we watched YouTube until we went to sleep. I had such a good day.

Leo Hollinshead (11)

Highfields Primary Academy, Highfields

The Incredible Diary Of Dr Maggie

Dear Diary,

The glimmering stars shone above me and I glanced around the empty room. I was alone in here. Everyone else was doing their thing so I caught a glimpse through the telescope. Suddenly I felt a pulse through my veins and I looked around me. I wasn't surrounded by the walls of the telescope, however. I was in space. The first thing I wanted to do was drive in a moon buggy! So I did. Next sliding on Saturn's wings I spotted a floating telescope. After peering through it I found myself back in the telescope room. Weird!

Nancy Pious (11)

Holy Cross Catholic Primary School, Leicester

Dr Maggie Aderin-Pocock's Space Adventure

Dear Diary,

I am stuck in a very complicated situation and I will explain now. I was going about my day and I helped to build, use and study the Gemini South telescope in Chile. I wanted to see how it felt to be in space so I started my journey. I entered the rocketship and started it up. When I entered space I looked around. I saw extraterrestrial beings coming out of a white hole. As I tried to escape, I entered a different galaxy known as the Andromeda galaxy. And that's it! I pray for my escape.

Jessika Rathinam (11)

Holy Cross Catholic Primary School, Leicester

The Incredible Diary Of How I Met My Best Friend

Dear Diary,
It was the first day back from the summer holiday. A girl called Oceanna, who was new, was scared so she hid in the cloakroom but then she came in and was seated next to me. I was shy like my name. She was sitting by herself on the wall at break time so I asked her to play. A year later we are still best friends. We never leave each other. When I don't come to school she wants to go home. That is the story of my magnificent, beautiful, caring best friend and my favourite person.

Shylah Mordarska (10)

Holy Cross Catholic Primary School, Leicester

The Wrath Of The Canyon

Dear Diary,

I was petrified. I crept to the edge of the canyon and I got across. A hunter helped me. It was the scariest moment of my life then he helped me up from the ground and welcomed me into his home. I was starving so I ate two meals of chicken korma, it was so marvellous.

I now live with them and I am now part of their tribe. I am very grateful and I am the happiest man alive.

It was nice meeting you. I'll update you later, bye.

Kaleb Melia (11)

Holy Cross Catholic Primary School, Leicester

Diary Of A Rainforest Explorer

Dear Diary,
Today I heard a noise outside my tent. I went outside to see what it was. It was a giant spotty cheetah. It was jumping on my tent. I screamed at the top of my lungs. Then I ran far away but it ran after me. He caught me and knocked me over. I was petrified. After that, he licked my face. I hope will visit me again. This has been the best day ever!

Lennon Watton (7)

Ladyloan Primary School, Arbroath

An Invitation

Dear Diary,

You wouldn't believe what happened today. As I was walking back from school I saw some owls. They were hooting loudly. Then one little brown owl flew down and perched on my shoulder. I was scared at first but then I realised it meant no harm. I saw something in its beak, it was a letter addressed to me. I wanted to open it there and then but I took it and ran home. It was an invitation to go to a magical world! Dare I go do you think dear diary? I have decided... I shall go!

Saira Hussein-Utley (9)

Morley Victoria Primary School, Morley

A Day In The Life Of Queen Elizabeth II

Dear Diary,
I wake up at 7:30am. Sometimes I stay in bed for a few minutes. I have my breakfast at 9am. Then my dogs get fed. then I go check on my horses, then I feed them. After that I go walk my dogs. When I get back I sit down for a minute. A few moments later I go dress my horses ready for their races. I watch them. Then I get them some water. A couple of hours later I go home, have tea, get my nightie on and go to bed.

Olivia Loney (9)
Morley Victoria Primary School, Morley

My Favourite Day

I like Tuesdays because we have computing. We learn everything about computing. It is fun and happens in my school. First time, I didn't know about computers. When I saw the computer room, I was very excited to do my work on my own computer. There are different apps. In the computer room, there is a different computer for each child. Everyone enjoys doing their own work. The teacher shows us on a computer and we have to copy this work on our own computer. Our teacher shows us good ways to use our computers and we save our work.

Mishal Aamir (8)
Mossford Green Primary School, Barkingside

Diary Of A Wimpy Kid Gets Rich Quick

Dear Diary,

I was at my unfriendly school when a huge group of bullies confronted me because I had a hole in my trousers. They called me nasty names and said I was *poor*. How could they?

Later that day, I was walking down the high street when I saw some lottery tickets. I didn't think. I snatched them and shoved them in my pocket. As soon as I got home, I watched on my TV and...

I won a million pounds!

The following day, the bullies came up to me and asked to be my friend. Um, aaah, *Nooo!*

Habiba Naeem (8)

Mossford Green Primary School, Barkingside

Voices In My Head

Dear Diary,

I am stuck in this game and I can't escape. My name is Figure and I keep hearing voices in my head. I am stuck in this scary mansion. Help me! From Figure.

Hasan Gunes (8)

Mossford Green Primary School, Barkingside

Mr Key

Inspired by Leaf by Sandra Dieckmann

Once, I got a headache and I saw a doctor called Doctor Key. He said, "To get the pain out, you have to shout stupid!"
"Ow! That made it worse."
The doctor said I could fight the pain away.
"Ow! I don't think this doctor knows what he's talking about! Wait a minute, Doctor Key, Doctor Donkey? Donkey. Donkey! Oh, it's gone, thanks Donkey."
He said, "You're welcome, Mason. If you need anything else, just ask me and come back in a month."
"Thanks again, bye-bye, annoying donkey!"
A singing donkey for the donkeys. I hate them very, very much!

Mason Cunningham (8)

Northcote Primary School, Liverpool

Wednesday's Trouble At School

Dear Diary,

Today, I went to a school called Northcote. Northcote was a strange school but that's where I found my best friend, Alexandra. She's in my class. But as the day passed, I began to get suspicious of a teacher. Suddenly, I found out that my teacher was a shapeshifter! The teacher's name was Mya Stanton and she changed into Miss Kelly.

At the end of the day, I went into my room and found my roommate and also my best friend. As I walked in, I saw a bright teddy and couldn't even breathe.

Iylah-May Cameron (9)

Northcote Primary School, Liverpool

Zeus, The God Of War

Hi, my name is Zeus. I am a powerful god. I look after Greece. I have electric powers and I've been a god for many centuries. I have a long white beard and my wife is called Leto. I'm kind but I'm protective over my family. I'm the father of all gods, humans and goddesses. I am the ruler of Olympus. My son is called Apollo and Artemis is his twin sister. I have defeated Typhon in a deadly battle. Everyone thinks they can beat me, but no one can. My pet is a giant golden eagle, my sacred animal.

Mason Stanton (8)

Northcote Primary School, Liverpool

Wednesday's Disaster

Dear Diary,

I was in the swimming baths when I saw someone who was wearing all black, like a full black costume and hair. Then she threw lots and lots of dangerous fish in the nice, spacious pool. While everyone was having fun, they swam towards the people in the pool. So they swam as fast as they could out of the pool because they would have been bitten. They all ran home as fast as they possibly could, so they did not get really, really badly hurt. They all got home safely to their families.

Kacy McHugh (9)

Northcote Primary School, Liverpool

The Polar Bear's Bad Month

Inspired by Leaf by Sandra Dieckmann

What a month I've had. I'm so glad to be home again with my family. It all started when I crossed the river and ended up in a scary, strange forest. I was desperate to get home and tried to fly by using lots of pretty leaves. Then I met some animals who made me feel blue. And then I became friends with some of the animals and I was happy.

Dennis Campbell (8)
Northcote Primary School, Liverpool

The Amazing Polar Bear

Inspired by Leaf by Sandra Dieckmann

Wow, what a day I've had! I'm so happy to be home again with my family. It started when I floated across the sea and ended up in a weird and wonderful forest. I was desperate to fly home, so I used lots of cute leaves. Then I met some animals who made me feel sad.

Heidi Livesy (9)

Northcote Primary School, Liverpool

I Turn My Teacher Into A Dwarf

Dear Diary,

I was walking to school and I saw a mysterious green glass bottle on the ground so I picked it up and put it in my bag.

So when I got to school I showed it to my teacher, Mrs Ward, and she took a drink and she turned into a small, tiny, slow, mysterious creature. So me and my class were scared so we ran outside and everyone was a dwarf.

Suddenly I saw an Ender portal so I ran into the Ender portal and that's all that I remember from that day!

Lexi Cummings (10)

Our Lady's RC Primary School, Perth

Running From Your Father

Dear Diary,

I woke up with a start. However, I couldn't fail to notice the deafening silence. It roamed around the room like a ghost. I tried to speak, but the only thing that came out my mouth was my cold breath. Five minutes later, I was ready to go to school (which I usually bunked) but when I walked to the door the silence struck me even more. I opened the door. Suddenly a great man stood before me. I ran for my life. Nevertheless, it came towards me. "Are you running from your father?" he cried. "Go, school!"

Wajeeh Ather (10)
Parkfield Primary School, Hendon

The Fear

I, Joe, awoke to a loud bark. I ran down the stairs frightened to see what was happening. Something was wrong, I knew this wasn't a dream. Carefully, still going and creeping downstairs, I was shocked by what I saw. My German Shepherd (which was trained) captured a fox which was trying to eat my rabbits that we bought just a week ago. The dog was feasting and eating the fox until only the remains of bones were left on the carpet. I was very pleased and told the dog, "Well done, boy!" My dog panted happily.

Darius Creivean (11)

Parkfield Primary School, Hendon

My Name Is God

In the beginning, I created Heaven and the Earth, also I separated the light from the darkness. The light I named 'day' and darkness I named 'night'. Everything I do for you, even the sky and the ocean. I commanded the Earth to produce all kinds of plants, those that bear grain and those that bear fruit. Then I commanded to let lights appear in the sky to separate day from night, they will shine in the sky to give light to the Earth I created all kinds of life but the best creation of all was the human.

Elias Vargas (10)
Parkfield Primary School, Hendon

SpongeBob's Adventure

Last year, I went to the beach in Spain where I spent all my holidays. One night, I dreamed I was SpongeBob who lives under the sea. In my house, I invited all my friends. The house was a giant pineapple. After that moment, I started inviting my friends such as Squidward, Gary and Patrick. We ate many things. Finally, we spent together a fantastic day. Really it was an exciting experience under the sea.

Nacer Agouni Tabac (10)
Parkfield Primary School, Hendon

The Largest Discovery In The World Of Apes

Dear Diary,

Today I met the most extraordinary creatures on Earth, some two-legged monsters but no powers. Crazy right, or is it that I don't know the world outside? That's what I asked myself, I mean I'm an ape with special blazing firepower living in the Amazon jungle! Of course, monsters and crocodiles arrive here, but they must be protected and I the guardian must complete my duty and I welcomed them into our wonderful home and recognised they walk with their legs just like me. There was a threat and they helped me but it was very dangerous.

Tesh Davies (9)
Pound Hill Junior School, Pound Hill

The Strange Day!

Dear Diary,

I woke up, as usual, yesterday and went to school. On the way home I went to the shops and I bought some chocolate and ate it. I opened my door and it broke. *That's odd*, I thought. When I was on my way to school today I clicked my finger and was in school. I teleported there quickly. *That was very odd*, I thought. In school today a large heavy rock appeared. I tried to push it and it worked. At break, I played football. I was a lot faster. I was so fast. A strange day!

Eesa Khan (9)

Pound Hill Junior School, Pound Hill

Dear Diary

Dear Diary,

Today I woke up and I brushed my teeth. I had breakfast and got ready for school but I couldn't find my teddy, Floppy, anywhere. I searched everywhere in my house. My brother had hidden it away. I went to school at 8am. I got out of the car at 8:17 when we were dropped off at the drop-off point at school. In school my friends and I planted cress. They grew big, strong and tall but some of mine were grown and some were not grown.

Angelina Wong (10)

Pound Hill Junior School, Pound Hill

Moon Lady

This is Moonlady and she lives on the moon.
One day she was coming home from the shops and she discovered Granny wasn't there. She looked everywhere but she couldn't find Granny. Then she found some footprints and followed them. Then they faded. "Oh no!" she cried.
Then she saw a light. She followed it and it led right to Granny but she was ill.
"Why are you ill?"
"Because it is getting colder, you know."
"What?" said Moonlady.
"Yes, it's true," said Granny.
Then Moonlady took Granny to the doctor. The doctor said, "Granny has got a cold. Yikes!"

Olive Massa (6)
Prendergast Ladywell School, Lewisham

The Day The Unicorn Lost Her Horn

A unicorn called Amelia lost her horn at the beach because she wanted to see the sunrise. A rock tripped her up and she lost her horn.

A mermaid saw the horn and grinned and said, "This can be on my crown and I will be the queen of the sea."

Then Amelia saw the unicorn. "What are you looking for?"

"My horn!"

She looked at the coral reef. "Hmmm, no horn." She saw a palace and swam inside and there was the crown! The mermaid gave it back.

"Please be my friend." They were best friends in the world.

Mimi Copeland (6)
Prendergast Ladywell School, Lewisham

Alexe Fisher's Diary

Dear Diary,

Today wasn't the day I had expected.

Hi, my name is Alexe and I get bullied a lot 'cause I'm in a wheelchair. But today everyone was nice. I was a little confused by the way they acted. So I went to Dan, he was my only friend, the one that cared for me.

Everyone would usually bully me so I went to the head teacher and he said, "Your parents came in." I was happy and relaxed now and felt like everyone else in the world and that's my story, bye.

Anika Paquete (11)

Prendergast Ladywell School, Lewisham

Journey Of My Dream

Dear Diary,

One sunny morning I woke up and got ready to move. I grabbed my items and we left for the little cottage. The cottage was surrounded with different wildlife animals and creatures.

"My mum is a vet," I said to my new friend, Aleena.

"I love wildness," she said. We went outside and played with the animals.

Thirty minutes later, my mum called us in and said, "Girls, come quick. An elephant is hurt."

We went racing inside to help. We fed some baby animals then went to bed.

"What a wonderful dream that was!" I said, joyfully.

Maymunah Basharat (9)

Riddlesden St Mary's CE Primary School And Nursery, Riddlesden

A Monster And A Boy Versus A Bully

Once there were two boys called Janis and Bob, they were both eight. Janis and Bob were both playing in the school playground when suddenly a boy called George started bullying them.

Bob started crying, so Janis said, "Stop bullying us," and then Bob and Janis ran away. Janis said to Bob, "Are you okay bestie?"

Then Bob replied, "Yes, thank you."

Then Janis walked over to George.

George said, "Why are you here?"

Then Janis replied, "*To do this!*"

Janis had turned into a big monster! Everyone in the school playground ran inside, including Bob. Bob was very mad.

Olivia Soulsby (9)

Springfield Primary Academy, Scartho

The Mysterious Monster Versus The Green Goblin

Dear Diary,

Once, on a Thursday, there was a battle that was a mysterious monster against the unstoppable Green Goblin in a maze. The maze was the world's largest maze, 2350 metres long and sixty feet tall. My best friend Logan and I watched it. The battle began at 2pm. The time was 2:05pm. The mysterious monster kept going to dead ends but was further and the Green Goblin kept going backwards. The time was 4pm. The mysterious monster had almost won. Without stopping, the mysterious monster claimed the champion title and was the greatest maze escaper in the world.

Harry Cook (9)

Springfield Primary Academy, Scartho

The Incredible Diary Of A Hamster

Dear Diary,
I woke up in the morning and crawled down the blue ramp. I saw my dull food bowl. I ate my fantastic, yummy food. I chugged my water. I ran super fast to my bright, shiny, green wheel. I ran for quite a long time.
Then I saw my owner and he let me play with him. I got lots of amazing strokes. It was one of the best days ever, except that one time when I got to play with loads of people.
I got put back into my cosy, warm cage. I crawled to bed. *Zzzzz.*

Harrison Mirrington (9)

St James' RC Primary School, Petts Wood

Beth Mead Meeting

Today I woke up in a field. I felt curious.

Someone gasped, "She's awake."

I started to open my eyes. Loads of people were running to me, "Are you okay? Are you hurt?"

I was about to say something before I realised it was a crowd of women in blue and white uniforms. They were football players.

"Are you in there?"

I saw that it looked like Beth Mead. I said, "Are you...?"

"Yes."

She knew I was a fan because I was wearing my England kit. "I can see you're a fan."

"Yep, I was feeling scared!"

"Sorry, love."

Eliza Beckett (9)

St John Vianney Catholic Primary School, St Helens

I Thought It Was A Normal Tuesday...

It was a normal Tuesday, well, I thought it was. I brushed my teeth at the exact same time and I had my breakfast. Pretty much everything was the same until lunchtime at the best school in the country.

We learned spells in class. Today we learned to say 'kapooza' to zap things and it really came in handy at lunchtime. At lunch, a rumbling sound occurred. Everyone could feel and hear it. Then the wizard headteacher came. He was envious of my school. When he rose he was facing the other way.

"That's it!" I screamed.

Temi Adesina (9)
St Joseph's Catholic Primary School, Northfleet

My New College

Today was a tough day because I was waiting for my taxi to bring me to college. It was really big! Some people showed me around (I felt nervous), it was very hot. I went outside and it was very big, I was in paradise. The teachers looked awesome. Maths was stressful, I was going to faint in ten minutes because it was so hot (and painful). I was very happy to be in college but I wanted my own studio and my taxi driver said he would get me my own studio. I was really excited to play here.

Jesleen Kaur (9)
St Mary's CE School, Norwood Green

The Space Park

Dear Diary,
Today I got launched into space as an experiment to see if you can play ice hockey in space. While we were playing ice hockey, someone miss-shot, and I was catapulted into the dark void of space. In the void, I was spinning and waving into a black hole but then got thrown out of the black hole by the infamous space worm but I didn't get sucked out of that. I saw the rocketship through the teeth of the space worm and it was coming towards me. I was so excited that I was saved. *Crash!*

Elias Boardmen (10)
St Mary's RC Primary School, Swinton

The Magic Necklace

Dear Diary,

Today was crazy. It was my 18th birthday. I was so excited. I woke up and went to eat my breakfast. I was expecting pancakes because that is what everyone wants on their birthday but today I had to make cereal by myself! They had forgotten my birthday! I went to think. I saw my friend, Dotty, only she understands me. She skipped towards me and gave me a gift. I opened it, a beautiful necklace lay inside. I was shocked. I found out that it was magic but never found out what the magic was.

Thea McNamara (10)
St Mary's RC Primary School, Swinton

My Life!

Dear Diary,

All my life I've felt alone and not like everyone in a bad way. I always feel like I don't belong anywhere and always feel excluded. I always listen to sad music and cry alone in my room. Sad stuff and more sad stuff, sometimes I do little acting things in my room to calm me down. I love acting and really want to do acting auditions. I want to be in a movie or Netflix series. I haven't told my mum but even as a nine-year-old I know what I want to do. My life is crazy!

Mollie Jones-Gore (9)
St Mary's RC Primary School, Swinton

Rocky's Glove

Dear Diary,

Today I hit Drago, he fell down and I won the fight by a knockout. It was so much fun and Rocky went up a mountain and shouted Drago at the top. Then my first fight against Spider. I won easily. Then Apollo Creed wanted to fight and I lost because of the judges. I then had a rematch and I won. I bit his hand like really hard and we both went down. I got up and won. I was proud of Rocky Balboa, really proud.

Yours sincerely, Rocky's Glove.

Maximus Jones (9)

St Mary's RC Primary School, Swinton

My Power

Dear Diary,
Today is the weekend so I wanted to go outside for a while and play in the snow. When I got my clothes on there wasn't any snow so I slammed my foot on the floor and when I did it started to snow. I thought it just randomly started to snow but I jumped and it instantly started to stop. I had a superpower. I was so excited I jumped so it started snowing. At school, on Monday everybody loved what I could do. The bullies stopped annoying me and everybody played. It was the best.

Isla Howard (7)

Stanion CE Primary School, Stanion

The Incredible Diary Of Brucie The Husky Dog

6am. I was fast asleep. Shake! Shake! *Oh no, help me. Heidi's forcing me to go on an early walk again. All I want to do is carry on dreaming!* I thought to myself.

"Here we go again. Round the block."

Eyelids shutting, pointy ears drooping, I could see my friends. They were also sleepy. I gave my friends a quiet woof.

"Time to go back home," muttered Heidi. "A nice big cup of tea for me."

I thought *yeah, finally! Home at last.*

I headed towards my cradle, closed my eyes and went back to sleep. Goodnight.

Heidi Peters (11)

Swallow Dell Primary School, Welwyn Garden City

The Girl Motorbike Races

There was this girl called Frankie. She loved riding motorbikes! For Christmas, she got a race bike. She thanked her dad. She was so pleased. So he told her the price, £2674. "Wow," she said. Frankie kept practising and practising and practising.

After two months of riding, her dad said, "Wanna earn some money?"

Frankie said, "Yes!"

So the first race was okay. But she got better, better and better. After playing around, time for riding. She kept doing it for years.

One day she came first place. She finally won £1759.

Frankie Myers (10)

Swallow Dell Primary School, Welwyn Garden City

A Tale Of Mystical Lands

Once upon a tale, there was a girl that loved to play hide-and-seek. Her favourite spot to hide was the closet. She played every day till one day her friend came down to play... She hid in her spot and waited.

Time went by and still nothing. She went out to check and nearly fainted. "It's like a dream!" she said, standing in a cloud of candyfloss with trees of Smarties and caramel apples. A path of bricks but it wasn't just bricks... it was gum! The path led to another closet gleaming white. She went and disappeared...

Saim Ahmed (11)

Swallow Dell Primary School, Welwyn Garden City

The Day My Family Got Eaten Alive

Dear Diary,

Today me and my family went on a trip to California but our dog Bow couldn't come so I am writing in here to pass the time. Oh! Also, my name is Danny. My parents' names are Emma and John. We are here! We stopped at a motel. I saw a pool so we took a dip in it but it turned out we climbed into a piranha tank. When we were out we had scratches and bites all over us so we went to bed and we'll leave another day.

Logan Kirton (10)
Swallow Dell Primary School, Welwyn Garden City

My Life As A Pencil

Dear Diary,

I was resting on a large, brown object when a rumble came into the room. I was picked up by a colossal giant and dragged across a white square! The huge giant drew with my head until I was blunt! Then he or she carried me to a round object and twisted! Before I knew it, I was thrown into the large, brown object. On top of me, I heard scrubbing. I got picked up again. Next to me, I saw a rectangular thing which was sitting there doing absolutely nothing. Suddenly, the huge giants ran out...

Rayyan Delawala (9)

The Chadderton Preparatory Grammar School, Chadderton

My Sister's Disaster Diary

Dear Diary,
I woke up today to find my clock wasn't working. I went downstairs to make my brother's birthday cake. Firstly, I didn't have enough ingredients so I had to make do. Then I burnt the silly cake. I got so angry I threw the cake at my brother's head. It exploded with a satisfying splat! Mum shouted at me so I went to my car and drove away in a huff. I was so cross I did not realise the roadworks and I drove through a red light. Then I ended up down the hole they made.

Samuel Murdock (10)
The Cope Primary School, Loughgall

Alien Day

Dear Diary,

On Wednesday there was an alien spaceship but it was not made of metal. It was made out of obsidian. As it hovered towards me, my body started changing colour like a rainbow and I felt stronger than ever. But I felt dead cold. Everyone started to throw knives towards it and one knife killed the engine. The ship exploded into smithereens and nothing was left but dead aliens. They took me to the hospital and I was asleep for eight months straight.

Max Cota (9)

The Erme Primary School, Ivybridge

My Day Out

Dear Diary,
Today I went to Crufts, it was so fun! In the beginning, I watched as children and dogs walked around an obstacle course.
When they finished, we went to see the terriers, like the Norfolk, Scottish and West Highland terriers. The cute dogs went on in rows. After the terriers, we went to the lunch stand where we could see London buses!
After lunch, we went to the main hall because we wanted to see all the cute dogs. So, Diary, how did you like Crufts? It was so fun.

Tristan Bishop (7)
The Gower School, Barnsbury

Ice Cream

I'm the creator of ice cream. I am really proud because millions of people love my invention. I made my invention in a factory and it was declared the first to make ice cream! It was a delicious invention and many people agree.

I was supposed to get invited to the Crystal Palace, but I wasn't alive. What an opportunity missed! I wish I was alive, it would have been such a privilege.

Ice cream is one of the biggest inventions of all time, in my opinion. Ice cream is as big today as it was back in my day.

Kian Singleton (11)
Unity Academy, Blackpool

John Logie Baird

Dear Diary,
Oh dear! Today was terrible! Disks everywhere, windows were broken, glass smashed, all around another failure. This is the second time this week. Now I have to make it again!
Maybe I should test it somewhere else, other than my house or garage. Maybe I should change my components for it. But maybe not. I don't know. I can't keep failing, but the thing to do is not give up.
Unless I have no choice but to give up. But there are many other reasons to keep trying.

Euan Mcgrandles (11)

Unity Academy, Blackpool

About Thomas Edison

Dear Diary,

I cannot believe how fast I made my invention work!

I was happy with my job, which was selling items, but sadly I lost all my jobs. This made me sad and desperate to find a job. But I had an idea: to make the world's first lightbulb without gas!

No one ever believed me but I never gave up. I saved a child and the father taught me how to do morse code, which helped. My chief believed me because he wanted to light up homes. It took me a while, but I finally did it!

Shreya Chemmaleth (10)

Unity Academy, Blackpool

John Logie Baird

Dear Diary,
Today was an eventful day. I was adding more to my TV in the comfort of my own home when a terrible accident happened. Who knew I was such a clumsy person?
All I needed to do was transport my TV across the room. It sounds so simple, right? Wrong! I was being so careful when, suddenly, I tripped over my own feet and dropped my precious work in the fire! It was terrible. I will never see the finished product!

Callum Carney (11)
Unity Academy, Blackpool

A Footballer

Dear Diary,

My dream as a young boy was to be a footballer and win the World Cup. I kept travelling and I kept getting better and then I got into a team and I scored my goals. I got 'man of the match'. I got my first trophy and then my second trophy and, as I got older I got into PSG and my dream came true. I was playing in the World Cup and I was in a penalty shoot-out. We won. My dream came true!

Charlie Bainbridge (10)
Wheatlands Primary School, Redcar

Day In The Life Of A Helpless Bin

Dear Diary,

Today was a tough day. People put rubbish inside me once again. This stuff needs to stop! It happens every day. Also an evil, disgusting seagull bumped into a man and he dropped his hot dog in me and now I am burnt like a crust. But luckily for me, it was a cold day. Then the seagull came back for round two... But he wasn't ready for this. Smoke, yeah... I don't want to talk about it!

Lucas McGivern (11)

Wheatlands Primary School, Redcar

Rubble The Puppy Dog

Dear Diary,

My name is Rubble. I went on the best walk with my owner, her name is Kaitlin. We went out to the woods with my ball, but then I saw a dog, the best thing in the world. We played and we sniffed, but then we had to go again. Kaitlin started to throw the ball but it was really far each time so I was very tired, but I kept going because it was so fun each time. The next one I got stuck in a hole, but I got out and now I am very happy!

Kaitlin Williamson (10)

Whitechapel CE Primary School, Cleckheaton

Space Trooper

One day a space trooper called George got a message on his iPad. When he turned it on there was no Wi-Fi because he lived in space. George was all alone. He had no friends. George lived on an airship far away from Earth. He grew up on the airship alone.

One night, he woke up to the sound of thunder, but then, *crash*, another airship hit his airship. He went to that ship and entered. He said, "Why did you blow up my ship?"

He said, "Sorry, but I was just looking for a friend." Then they were friends.

Jacob Leenhouwers (8)

Wrockwardine Wood CE Junior School, Trench

A Day In The Life Of Flicka The Fantastical Dog

Dear Diary,

At the start of the day, I got out of my crate and slept some more on the sofa. I got woken up by the girls getting ready for school. I joined a snowball fight with some of them. Sometime later, I went on a walk with my adoptive mother and sister. I came back to go to bed at this time to sleep a bit more. Because it was snowing hard, they all came back! I drove in the car for hours, the others teleported or something! I had food and then went to bed. Zzzzz.

Eira Lewis (10)
Ysgol Gymraeg Y Fenni, Abergavenny

YOUNG WRITERS INFORMATION

We hope you have enjoyed reading this book – and that you will continue to in the coming years.

If you're the parent or family member of an enthusiastic poet or story writer, do visit our website **www.youngwriters.co.uk/subscribe** and sign up to receive news, competitions, writing challenges and tips, activities and much, much more! There's lots to keep budding writers motivated!

If you would like to order further copies of this book, or any of our other titles, then please give us a call or order via your online account.

Young Writers
Remus House
Coltsfoot Drive
Peterborough
PE2 9BF
(01733) 890066
info@youngwriters.co.uk

Join in the conversation!
Tips, news, giveaways and much more!

 **YoungWritersUK**   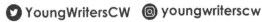 **YoungWritersCW**    **youngwriterscw**

Scan to watch the
Incredible Diary Video

YoungWriters®
— Est. 1991 —